Twilight

Atheneum Books for Young Readers
An imprint of Simon & Schuster Children's Publishing Division
1230 Avenue of the Americas
New York, New York 10020

Book design by Angela Carlino
The text of this book is set in Baskerville BE.
The illustrations are rendered in watercolor.
Printed in Hong Kong
2 4 6 8 10 9 7 5 3 1

Library of Congess Cataloging-in-Publication Data
Huth, Holly.
Twilight / by Holly Huth ; illustrated by David McPhail. — 1st ed.
p. cm.
Summary : A little girl takes charge of bringing on the twilight, that time
of day that it begins to turn to night.
ISBN 0-689-81975-7 (alk. paper)
[1. Twilight–Fiction. 2. Night–Fiction.] I. McPhail, David M., ill.
II. Title.
PZ7.H9647Tw 1999
[E]–dc21 98-19067
CIP
AC

FIRST

EDITION

David McPhail

Twilight

written by Holly Young Huth

Atheneum Books for Young Readers

NEW YORK LONDON TORONTO SYDNEY SINGAPORE

$\mathcal{T}$he little girl took charge of the day as it turned into night. Up along the avenue she skipped in a zigzag, merry way.

"It's twilight," she shouted to her mother.
"It's twilight," she said to the man in the
store window and to the people she passed
on their way home from work. "Twilight,
twilight, twilight," the little girl announced
to the city.

"She's the keeper of twilight," her mother explained as they sped by a couple in love, who were laughing.

Up beyond the tall buildings the
sky was not a color you could say,
but it was soft. And it held fast to its
light as if waiting for permission to
be night. And then the pink came . . .

The little girl threw her head back
to take it all in. "It's twilight!" she
shouted again, reminding the world
in case it forgot.

With a wave of her hand across the sky, it began. She'd be the one to lead the way. She was the keeper of twilight.

"I'm in charge of the twilight here and there and everywhere," the little girl keeper announced. "Now I must go to the faraway places to check on the time that comes before dark."

And she lifted up and up and up . . .
to a place that lived after the sun and
before the moon. She went straight
through a crack where the sky stood
still to the quiet world of twilight.

First she climbed her way up to the faint
day stars and helped them get ready to shine.
But she reminded them as she went away,
"It's not time."

Just as the sun was tucking itself in under the woolly hills, she read it a bedtime story.

When a coyote pack howled through the desert silence, the little girl ran over and hushed them up. "Not yet," she said, "not yet."

She scolded an owl for opening an eye. "It's too soon," she said, "too soon."

She flew for a while with a flock of pelicans
on their way home for supper . . . down through
the darkening sky.

That's when she found the moon, hiding behind the ocean, and persuaded it to rise.

On the way home she saw a man in a window, straining to read his newspaper, and she flicked on the light behind him.

Before she knew it, she was back on the sidewalk again, just in time to see the lights of the city sparkle all at once like a thousand dressed-up stars.

Reaching for her mother's hand, the little girl whispered, "It's nighttime now."

She wasn't in charge of that.